W9-AWL-149

STAR WARS™

R2-D2 AND X-WING

a division of

INSIGHT EDITIONS

San Rafael, California

STAR WARS

R2-D2

AN INSIDE LOOK AT THE ULTIMATE ASTROMECH DROID

BY MICHAEL KOGGE

INTRODUCTION

The diminutive astromech droid known as R2-D2 may not look like much, but he's one of the toughest, most versatile droids ever to roll on three legs. He can pilot starships, carry out complicated repairs, record messages, and even play holochess. Over his long and storied career, R2 has managed to avoid system resets to develop a quirky personality and an independent mindset. This can make him a frustrating coworker yet the most endearing of companions.

Some engineers say a sense of humor can never be programmed, but that has never stopped R2-D2 from developing one. While his counterpart C-3PO believes suffering to be their lot in life, R2-D2 seems quite content to chirp merrily (or rudely) at whatever challenges the galaxy throws at him. His devil-may-care attitude often gets him into trouble but at the same time gives him the key to getting out of it. Experience has trained his logic circuits that the quickest route out of a jam is to compute new and seemingly illogical ways of employing his equipment. R2-D2 has learned that his gadgets best serve him in situations that don't match their manufacturers' specifications.

R2-D2's role in galactic events may have inflated his digital ego—at least according to C-3PO—but it has not changed his devotion to his comrades. It's rare to find a droid as loyal and reliable as R2-D2, even if he can be persnickety and stubborn at times. Numerous upgrades over the years keep R2 humming along with the latest models while other units of his age have been resigned to the trash compactor. As long as his friends still need him, R2-D2 will always have the pluck and resourcefulness to keep rolling on and never become obsolete.

BASIC CAPABILITIES

Primarily engineered for astronavigational assistance and starship maintenance, R2-D2 also doubles as a general-purpose utility droid. His functionality extends to holographic recording, image projection, data storage, fire extinguishing, and sensor scanning. He's even been known to serve drinks, proving he fits his manufacturer's famous advertising slogan: "No job is over this little guy's head."

TECHNICAL SPECIFICATIONS

MANUFACTURER: Industrial Automation

MODEL: R2 series

DROID CLASS: Two

HEIGHT: 1.09 m (3 ft, 6 in)

COST: 5,000 Imperial credits for starter model

COMMUNICATION MODULE: Binary (droidspeak)

GENDER MODULE: Male

TRIPODAL DESIGN

Three hydraulic legs permit a sturdy, upright position on a variety of surfaces for all-terrain maneuverability. Two of the legs are always operational, while the middle leg can be extended for extra stability or retracted for speed.

MOTORIZED ROLLER TREAD: Mobility controlled by powerbus cables

MAGNETIC LOCK: For firm attachment to starship hulls

RADAR EYE: Photoreceptor can monitor and measure the visible, infrared, and electromagnetic spectra

PROCESSOR STATE INDICATOR: Displays performance of internal systems

POWER CELLS: Can energize movement, even if body or brain is disabled

HOLOCAM ACCESSORIES

The astromech can capture and show moments in time, making him an ideal messenger.

CAMERA: Radar eye records full three-dimensional figures.

ROTATING PROJECTOR: Can be aimed to display holographic messages and broadcasts in sizes suited to the surrounding environment and audience

PERISCOPE SYSTEM: R2-D2 has multiple antennae that provide visual and biochemical data.

AUDITORY MICROPHONES: Distinguish important sounds from a range of environmental noise

SENSORY INPUT

R2-D2's full-service sensor package includes a number of features.

ELECTROMAGNETIC SENSOR UNIT: Measures surrounding electromagnetic spectrum

DROID OF ALL TRADES

R2-D2 is not your ordinary, off-the-rack astromech. Over his many years in operation, R2 has acquired an array of assorted gadgetry that would seem ill-serving for a droid of his class. Yet all of these instruments have come in handy at one point or another—and are often used in a manner their designers never dreamed!

PERISCOPE (ENVIRONMENTAL SCANNER): Detects life-forms and examines air content through basic chemical analysis

MISCELLANEOUS TOOLS

R2-D2 hosts many other features that few know about until he calls them into action.

PERISCOPE (VISUAL DATA): Extendable above dome for a 360-degree view and sweep of surroundings, with signal booster

ELECTRIC PROD: When R2 requires a zap to get things going, this packs quite a charge.

UNIVERSAL EXTENDER ARM: Can be fitted with a wide array of tips, from computer interface prongs to saws and manipulators of various sizes.

COMPUTER INTERFACE: One of R2's most used implements is his computer interface tool, which plugs into dataports for exchanging information.

DATA CARD READER: Accepts a degree of shapes, sizes, and formats, from data-tapes to holodiscs

EMITTER NOZZLE: Located under hinged dome panel; sprays either fire extinguishing foam or vent fumes to create a smoke screen

ATTITUDE JETS: Propel R2-D2 through space and atmospheres

GRIPPER: Pincers give R2-D2 the ability to grab and manipulate exterior objects.

ARMS

A carousel of internal rotating appendages extends from R2-D2's dome and cylindrical body. Various fittings like welding tips, cutting saws, and even beverage dispensers can expand an arm's utility for almost any purpose.

FEARLESS FLYER

Despite possessing three legs, R2-D2 was designed for duties off the ground. He's at home in the rear socket of a starfighter, has no qualms making extravehicular repairs in space, and can even fly all on his own when needed.

COURAGEOUS COPILOT

Any account of the legendary piloting of Luke Skywalker and his father Anakin would be incomplete without mention of their astromech droid. Though Jedi reflexes give Luke and Anakin an incredible advantage in space battles, they would be lost if not for R2-D2's invaluable assistance. While they do the breakneck flying, R2 crunches the numbers. His duties are numerous and require true versatility.

SYSTEMS STATUS: In conjunction with a starship's computers, R2 maintains a vigilant watch on the functionality of all components, including weapons, in order to carry out immediate repairs or boost power to different systems.

BATTLE ANALYSIS: Studying a space engagement from multiple angles and data sources, R2 estimates best-case scenarios an provides telemetry and guidance to the pilots.

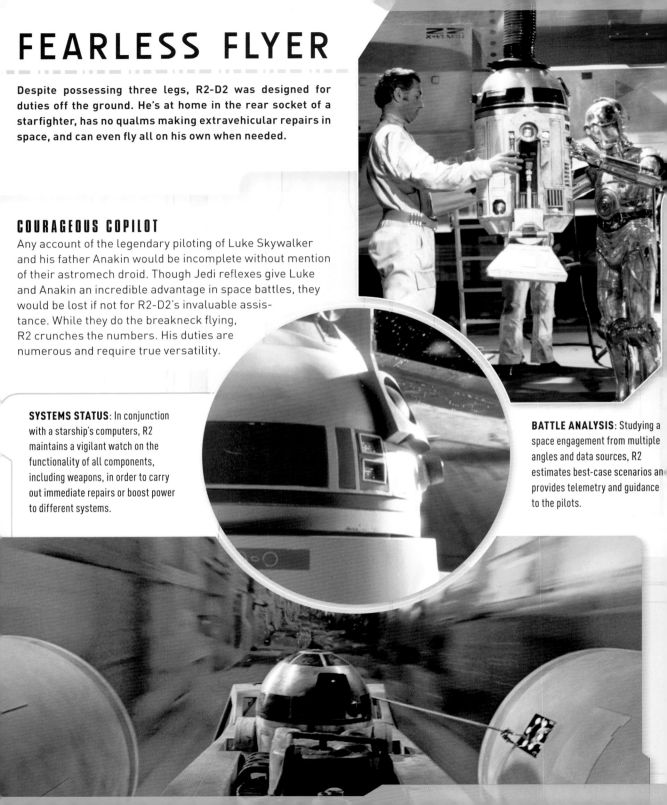

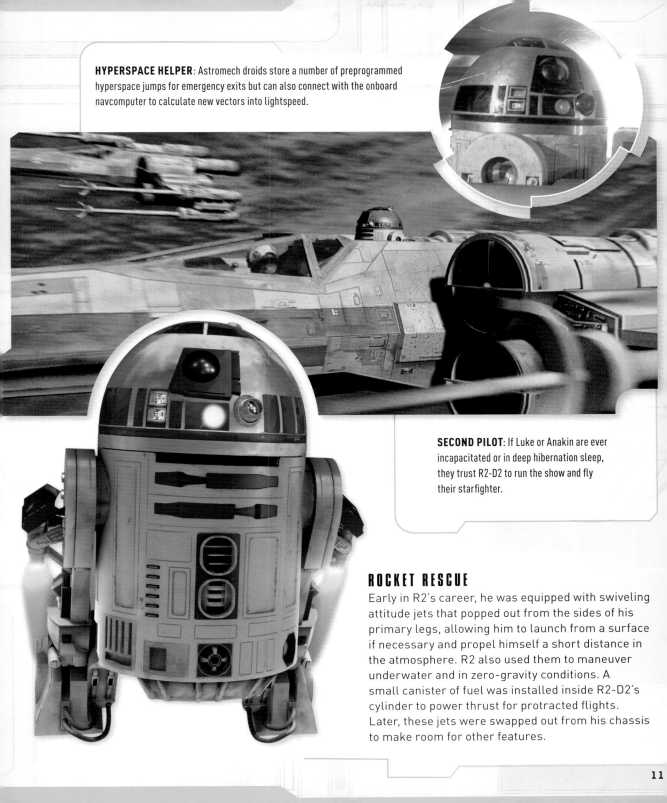

HYPERSPACE HELPER: Astromech droids store a number of preprogrammed hyperspace jumps for emergency exits but can also connect with the onboard navcomputer to calculate new vectors into lightspeed.

SECOND PILOT: If Luke or Anakin are ever incapacitated or in deep hibernation sleep, they trust R2-D2 to run the show and fly their starfighter.

ROCKET RESCUE

Early in R2's career, he was equipped with swiveling attitude jets that popped out from the sides of his primary legs, allowing him to launch from a surface if necessary and propel himself a short distance in the atmosphere. R2 also used them to maneuver underwater and in zero-gravity conditions. A small canister of fuel was installed inside R2-D2's cylinder to power thrust for protracted flights. Later, these jets were swapped out from his chassis to make room for other features.

CANTANKEROUS COUNTERPARTS

Though R2-D2 and C-3PO are droids, they have somehow overridden their programming to become the greatest of friends. The evidence is in their behavior. They bicker and quarrel endlessly, often tramping or trundling away from each other in a huff. Their petty disputes can make them highly inefficient—sometimes to the point where their owners have threatened to fit them with restraining bolts. Yet whenever one of them is in danger, the other hazards his circuits to make sure that their companion is safe. Theirs is an unbreakable bond that survives even memory wipes.

FIRST IMPRESSIONS

R2-D2 initially encountered a semi-assembled C-3PO in Anakin Skywalker's bedroom on Tatooine. His first beep to C-3PO caused the protocol droid some embarrassment as R2 announced that "his parts" were showing.

PROUD PARTNERS

After Anakin Skywalker fell on the volcanic plains of Mustafar and Padmé Amidala lost her life, R2-D2 and C-3PO found themselves under the supervision of a single master, Senator Bail Organa. Thus began their official association as counterparts.

KEPT SECRETS

A recalcitrant R2-D2 left his golden friend in Tatooine's Dune Sea in order to embark on a secret mission he refused to explain. C-3PO eventually found R2 in a Jawa sandcrawler and vouched for the droid's usefulness to Luke Skywalker.

HEAD HAULER

When C-3PO's head got attached to a battle droid's body amid a fierce fight between Jedi and Separatists on Geonosis, R2-D2 wheeled into the fray, attached a cable to the protocol droid's head, and then wrenched it off and towed it to safety.

THE THINGS I DO FOR YOU

After C-3PO was blasted into spare parts on Cloud City and experienced the distress of Chewbacca's hasty reassembly, R2-D2 repaired the protocol droid to full functionality.

FRIENDLY SHOVE

R2-D2 gave a nervous C-3PO a forceful bump off Jabba's soon-to-blow sail barge, saving his counterpart from being caught in the explosion.

HERO OF THE REPUBLIC

R2-D2's feats of bravery during the waning years of the Republic demonstrate that courage is not a quality limited to flesh-and-blood heroes.

INVASION OF NABOO
R2-D2 distinguished himself while serving in Queen Amidala's retinue.

FOCUSED FIXER: While Trade Federation battleships blasted his astromech compatriots, R2-D2 stayed firm to the hull of the queen's Royal Starship and repaired the vessel's shield generator so it could escape through the planetary blockade of Naboo. The Queen later honored R2—a rare distinction for a droid.

BACKSOCKET 'BOT: R2-D2 assisted nine-year-old Anakin Skywalker in flying a Naboo N-1 starfighter and destroying the Trade Federation control ship. The feat deactivated the battle droids on Naboo's surface, ending the occupation.

REPUBLIC IN PERIL

When the Separatists threatened the galaxy, R2-D2 remained in the charge of Anakin Skywalker and joined the budding Jedi Knight on many perilous quests.

POLITICAL PATROL: After a failed assassination attempt on Padmé Amidala's life, R2-D2 watched over the senator in her bedchamber and accompanied Anakin in guarding her during their trip to Naboo.

SENATOR SAVIOR: R2-D2 fired his booster rockets to fly through the droid factory on Geonosis. Finding Padmé trapped inside an empty vat, R2-D2 deposited himself near a terminal port. He issued a command to halt the molten ore from being poured into the vat, then rotated the vat so Padmé could escape.

BUZZ BEATER:
During the starfighter battle over Coruscant, R2-D2—plugged into the socket of Anakin Skywalker's Jedi interceptor—fended off a buzz droid and fed the Jedi Knight accurate telemetry to help turn the tide of the conflict.

BATTLE BLAZER: In the hangar of General Grievous's dreadnought, R2-D2 showered two super battle droids with flammable lubricant, which he ignited with his booster jets. Once free, he carried out Anakin Skywalker's commands to operate the turbolift so his master could save Chancellor Palpatine.

HERO OF THE REBELLION

R2-D2 may not have been able to prevent the fall of the Republic, but he was instrumental in defeating the Galactic Empire.

DEATH STAR DROID

If not for R2-D2, the Rebel Alliance might have been helpless against the Empire's first Death Star.

MEMORY MODULE: Princess Leia Organa of Alderaan stored the technical readouts to the Death Star battle station inside the memory banks of R2-D2. She also commanded him to fulfill a top-secret mission on Tatooine: Find the desert hermit Obi-Wan Kenobi and deliver the Death Star plans to the Rebel Alliance.

TRASH TALKER: R2-D2 communicated with the Death Star's computers to shut down all garbage compactors on the detention levels, thereby saving his new master Luke Skywalker and his friends from being flattened.

IMPERIAL RETALIATION

Though obsolete compared to other models, R2-D2 continued to serve Luke Skywalker, even when the Empire was on the verge of vanquishing the Rebels for good.

DAGOBAH DRIFTER: R2-D2 journeyed with Luke to the mysterious Dagobah system, where he provided company for his master and watched over the swamped X-wing fighter.

CLOUD CREATOR: Cut off from his master on Cloud City, R2-D2 ran into C-3PO and his other friends while they were being pursued by stormtroopers. R2-D2 fired his fire extinguisher toward the troopers, producing a smoke screen so the rebels could get away.

REBIRTH OF THE JEDI

Never showing his age, R2-D2 witnessed the fall of the Jedi and the rise of a new hope for their ancient order.

DRINK DISPENSER: Jabba the Hutt's supervisor droid, EV-9D9, fitted the astromech unit for a task that was an insult to R2-D2's design: serving beverages for the scum and villainy on the crime lord's sail barge. Nonetheless, R2 used this opportunity to serve something much more important—he supplied Luke Skywalker with his lightsaber.

SNARE SLICER: Caught in an Ewok net with his rebel friends, R2-D2 sawed through the ropes and released them. Unfortunately, his actions did not save them from being tied up on poles to be roasted over an Ewok fire!

ASTROMECH ANTICS

R2-D2's singular moments extend well beyond his time in the socket of a starfighter.

FUNNY FELLOW

Even in the darkest hour, R2-D2 always finds a way to lighten the mood.

WITTY WARBLER: R2-D2 manages to express his intentions with just hoots and whistles. Yet those who understand his binary droidspeak are often amused and astonished at R2's devious sense of humor. The little droid can cut someone down to size in a few beeps.

DISTRACTION DROID: When General Grievous captured Anakin, Obi-Wan, and Chancellor Palpatine aboard his flagship, R2-D2 drew attention to himself by putting on an incredible sound-and-light display. This diversion gave Obi-Wan the chance to summon his lightsaber from Grievous and free himself and Anakin from their bonds.

EWOK ELECTRIFIER: Being tied to a roasting spit by Ewoks does not make for a happy droid. Once released, R2-D2 showed his gratitude by zapping the furry natives with his power probe.

MISHAP MACHINE

Though he delights in pointing out C-3PO's embarrassments, R2-D2 is not without some of his own.

JAWA JITTER: The Jundland Wastes on Tatooine are not a safe place for a solitary astromech unit rolling along on a secret mission. One shot of a stun gun caused R2 to shake and fall forward on his radar eye, making him easy pickings for Jawa scavengers.

BOG BELCH: When the murky swamps of Dagobah proved deeper than R2-D2's height, the droid raised his periscope eye above water level. What he didn't see was the beast swimming behind him with an open mouth. Fortunately, metal robots don't serve as a tasty meal, and the creature spat R2-D2 toward dry land.

R-SERIES

R2-D2 hails from a very successful line of R-series astromech droids designed and manufactured by Industrial Automaton. His galactic journeys have crisscrossed with many of his mechanical cousins, some of whom bear his likeness with subtle differences.

ROYAL NABOO SECURITY FORCES

Naboo's security chiefs invested heavily in acquiring a large quantity of cutting-edge astrodroids for their N-1 starfighters.

R2-A6 – Assigned to *Bravo 1*'s Ric Olié, the personal pilot for Queen Amidala and commander of the Naboo Royal Space Fighter Corps.

R2-C4 – Had panels the color of straw and was often socketed in *Bravo 6*.

QUEEN AMIDALA'S PERSONAL RETINUE

These droids had the distinction of serving aboard the queen's Royal Naboo Starship. Along with R2-D2, they braved fire from the Trade Federation to venture out onto the hull and make repairs. Sadly, only R2-D2 survived.

R2-M5 – Had a paint scheme similar to R2-D2 but with maroon trim.

R2-B1 – Boasted bright yellow panels and a royal blue body.

R2-R9 – Featured both a red body and trim.

G8-R3 – Possessed the main body unit of an R2-series droid topped by a flattop head.

INDEPENDENT OPERATORS

A few astrodroids have lost their owners and are left to find their own way in the galaxy.

R3-T7 – A malfunctioning, blast-scorched yellow-and-green-paneled astromech who roams the upper levels of Coruscant, forever searching for his master.

R2-A5 – A green-and-white unit last seen trundling the streets of Mos Eisley on Tatooine.

R3-T2 – Also a resident of Mos Eisley, bearing a red dome and a white body.

JEDI DROID POOL

The Jedi maintained their own contingent of astro-mechs primed for communal use.

R4-P17 – This red-domed unit often accompanied Obi-Wan Kenobi on missions during the Clone Wars. She tracked Jango Fett's *Slave I* to Geonosis and fought with Kenobi during the Battle of Coruscant, where buzz droids brought her to an unfortunate end.

R4-G9 – Trimmed in bronze, R4-G9 also saw action with Obi-Wan Kenobi during the Clone Wars. She piloted Kenobi's Eta-2 fighter away from Utapau so that Kenobi's presence on the planet remained unknown while he hunted for General Grievous.

R4-P44 – Flew an ARC-170 starfighter as part of Obi-Wan Kenobi's clone trooper detachment.

REBEL ROBOTS

The R2-series' quirky personality seems to lend these units naturally to freedom fighters.

R2-X2 – A white-and-green striped unit on the X-wing *Red 10* who was destroyed during the Battle of Yavin.

R3-A2 – An orange-paneled, clear-domed droid who was posted to the rebel base on Hoth.

R3-Y2 – A Hoth command center droid who helped the rebels evacuate from the ice world.

INQUISITIVE IMPERIALS

The Galactic Empire has thousands of R2 astromechs in its service. Often they are painted in a stark black-and-white scheme.

R2-Q2 – A member of the boarding party that captured the Alderaanian cruiser *Tantive IV*.

R3-T6 – Clear-domed with red trim, this droid had astronavigational duties on the first Death Star.

R2-Q5 – Stationed on the second Death Star, R2-Q5 had a polished black body and bronze paneling.

BEHIND THE SCENES

"Artoo is the unsung hero of the two trilogies. He's the only one who knows the whole story."
—*Star Wars* creator George Lucas

FASCINATING FIRSTS

❯ One movie myth long bandied about was that the name "R2-D2" originated from the shorthand heading on a "Reel 2, Dialogue 2" editing cue sheet for Lucas's earlier film, *THX 1138*. In actuality, Lucas invented the name because he liked its phonetic pronunciation.

❯ Concept artist Ralph McQuarrie designed the look of R2 from Lucas's own notes, adding multiple retractable arms as if the cylindrical repair droid was a robotic Swiss Army knife!

BEEPING 'BOT

❯ The noises babies make inspired sound designer Ben Burtt to create R2-D2's vocal palette. He recorded himself making the sounds and then electronically processed them for playback on a synthesizer.

❯ In early drafts of the *Star Wars* screenplay, R2-D2 didn't beep in binary at all but had actual dialogue!

INSIDE THE CAN

❯ For the original *Star Wars* film, production designer John Barry designed R2's body so the actor Kenny Baker could fit inside. Baker would rotate the dome and bounce the body, animating the droid as if it were alive.

❯ Though radio-controlled R2 units were used in the original trilogy, advancements in technology later permitted greater mobility and expressiveness. By the time *Revenge of the Sith* was made, a human no longer manipulated the robot internally. R2-D2 was either remotely controlled by droid builder Don Bies or created using computer-generated imagery.

TOP LEFT: Kenny Baker enjoys a moment of Tunisian sun on the *Star Wars* shoot as his R2 unit is fixed for the cameras. LEFT: A crew member presents the R2 chassis to actor Kenny Baker.

TOP: Ralph McQuarrie's original concept painting featuring the droids with a sleek, *Metropolis*-inspired look.
ABOVE: A preproduction design sketch by Ralph McQuarrie shows R2's inner workings.

ABOVE: The *Star Wars* production team assists R2-D2 operator Kenny Baker and C-3PO actor Anthony Daniels during a key scene from *Empire Strikes Back*.

BELOW: Joe Johnston created this early concept illustration showing the droids after being jettisoned from Jabba the Hutt's sail barge in *Return of the Jedi*.

ABOVE: A proud Kenny Baker watches R2-D2 roll off on his own on the set of *The Phantom Menace*.

ABOVE: A young George Lucas with an early R2-D2 prototype.

INTERVIEW WITH A DROID WRANGLER

DON BIES, A FORMER SPECIAL EFFECTS ENGINEER AT INDUSTRIAL LIGHT AND MAGIC (ILM), SERVED AS THE DROID UNIT SUPERVISOR ON THE *STAR WARS* PREQUELS. HE SHARES HIS EXPERIENCES FOR FELLOW R2 MODEL MAKERS.

HOW DID YOU FIRST BECOME INVOLVED WITH R2-D2?

When the original film came out, I built my own R2-D2—full-size and remote-controlled. Fast forward ten years, and I had moved to Northern California and was working in the film industry. I crossed paths with David Schaeffer, who Lucasfilm hired to operate one of the original radio-controlled R2s for personal appearances. David left to work at Disney as an Imagineer, so his droid position was open. I talked to those in charge, and R2 and I began working together. Our first job was a campaign for Panasonic in Japan.

HOW DID THIS LEAD TO BECOMING THE MAIN "PUPPETEER" FOR R2-D2 IN EPISODE I?

When they began production on *The Phantom Menace*, they shipped all the R2s (there were about sixteen) to the UK for filming. They began having some issues with things like controlling him on sandy surfaces. Since I had a twelve-year history with R2 (along with two colleagues I brought in to help, Nelson Hall and Grant Imahara), producer Rick McCallum called me from England one day to discuss the challenges they were facing. It was decided at that meeting that we would put together a team at ILM to create a new R2 unit that could overcome some of the issues. We created an R2 with a much stronger drive system and a little camera to operate it remotely. Once finished, I accompanied it to the UK for filming and spent six weeks on set. When I returned, I operated R2 for added shots at ILM. When *Attack of the Clones* rolled around, filming was moved to Sydney, Australia, and Rick asked me to head up the crew.

HOW DID YOU "ACT" VIA REMOTE CONTROL?

The movements of the radio-controlled R2 are very basic, so there was not much of a challenge "acting." If he was to be excited in a scene, I'd just make him more jumpy by rattling the joystick more—it wasn't the same caliber as Alec Guinness's acting!

CAN YOU DESCRIBE HOW THE TECHNOLOGY ADVANCED FROM THE ORIGINAL TRILOGY INTO AND THROUGH THE PREQUELS?

Essentially, we tried to make everything simpler—I felt that the simpler things were, the less there would be to repair if it broke down. We upgraded all the electronics but used the same motors that were installed from the days of *The Empire Strikes Back*. We created a quick change battery pack system so that the batteries could be replaced in about thirty seconds. Overall, the units were much more reliable, but that was mainly due to the advances in remote control technology.

WHY WAS R2'S PAINT SCHEME DIFFICULT TO REPLICATE FROM THE ORIGINAL TRILOGY? WHAT TIPS MIGHT YOU GIVE INCREDIBUILDS MODEL MAKERS?

For the original film, the creators used a type of semi-transparent blue paint that allowed the surface underneath to come through. Because of that style of paint, it was very difficult to nail down the color of blue—it would look very different in various types of light. For *The Phantom Menace*, the UK artists simply painted it

a flat blue. I wanted to bring the original color back as close as possible because I felt it really added to the character. It took a lot of experimentation to come up with a recipe that was close.

For those trying to replicate it, it's best to build up layers with a transparent royal blue over a shiny chrome or aluminum base. There are two stage paints commercially available that would get very close to the color.

SINCE YOU'VE SPENT SO MUCH TIME WITH R2 AND C-3PO, WHAT DO YOU THINK MAKES THEM TICK? WHY HAVE THEY MADE SUCH AN INDELIBLE MARK IN POPULAR CULTURE?

It's been said so many times, but they are archetypes. They provide comic relief, but they are actually well-drawn characters and really serve a purpose in the story, especially in the original films. And I also believe it's a great testament to the performers from the first films—Anthony Daniels really brings C-3PO to life, and the combination of effects techniques creates R2's character. Kenny Baker adds a human element to his subtle movements, and Ben Burtt's sound design creates R2's soul. All together, they have made for memorable characters.

MAKE IT YOUR OWN

One of the great things about IncrediBuilds models is that each one is completely customizable. The untreated natural wood can be decorated with paints, pencils, pens, beads, sequins—the list goes on and on!

Before you start building and decorating your model, though, read through the included instruction sheet so you understand how all the pieces come together. Then, choose a theme and make a plan. Do you want to make an exact replica of R2-D2 or something completely wacky? The choice is yours! Here are some examples to get those creative juices flowing.

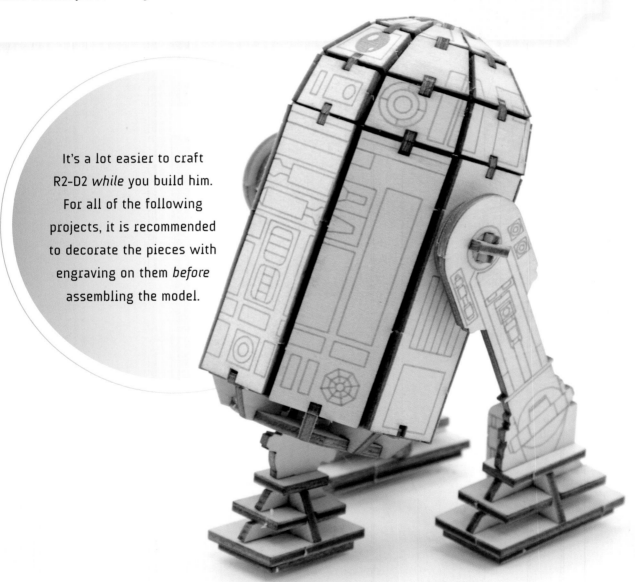

It's a lot easier to craft R2-D2 *while* you build him. For all of the following projects, it is recommended to decorate the pieces with engraving on them *before* assembling the model.

R2-D2 REPLICA

When making a replica, it's always good to study an actual image of what you are trying to copy. Look closely at details and brainstorm how you can re-create them. R2-D2 is a very detailed model, so take your time and be patient.

TIP: It's helpful to use colors in order from light to dark.

WHAT YOU'LL NEED:
- Blue, silver, white, and red paint
- Small paintbrush

OPTIONAL:
- Detail paintbrush (such as a 18/0 spotter)
- Small, flat bright brush (recommended 1/8″)
- Painter's or model tape

1. Start painting the engraved pieces with everything that should be white. Edge around details carefully. Let dry.

2. Paint in the silver where you want it to go. Let dry.

3. Paint in the blue where you want it to go, and add a final dab of red on R2-D2's front light.

4. After the engraved pieces are dry, assemble the model.

5. Finally, you can paint whatever is left— mainly R2-D2's legs and edges.

TIP: If you're having trouble making the lines straight, use a piece of painter's tape as a stencil. Simply tape around the area you want, and then paint inside. Wait until the paint is dry, and then lift up the tape. Voila!

MAKE IT YOUR OWN

R2-D2 IN THE SWAMPS OF DAGOBAH

You can also try re-creating R2-D2 in a specific scene from the *Star Wars* films. Here is R2-D2 as he emerges from the swamps of Dagobah on his mission to find Yoda with Luke Skywalker.

WHAT YOU'LL NEED:
- White, blue, and red colored pencils
- White, dark green, and brown paint
- Silver marker
- Paintbrush

OPTIONAL:
- An old dry paintbrush with rough bristles

For this model, you need to start with the R2-D2 Replica (page 29). A mixture of colored pencils and paint were used. (Colored pencils can make it easier to color in the details of the model.)

1. Follow steps 1 to 3 of the R2-D2 Replica. Replace paint with colored pencils and markers, but follow the same order of colors.

2. You can do one of two things next: Color the rest of the pieces with colored pencils, or assemble the model and use white paint to finish the edges and R2-D2's legs. White paint was used for this example.

3. Dab green and brown paint over the bottom half of the model. Don't be afraid to experiment! Use an old dry paintbrush with just a little paint for a speckled look. Press harder for more "blobs of mud." Layer the colors on top of each other. You can even blend some of the paint with your finger.

4. The top half of R2-D2 should be less swampy but still dirty. You'll want to carefully use your brush to drag some of the paint onto R2's top half. Sparser speckles work better than blobs here. You may even want to blend your brown paint with a little white to achieve a lighter effect.

5. Take your paintbrush and carefully dab more brown paint onto R2-D2's head. You don't want to overdo it, so be sparing.

Once you've achieved the look you want, you are finished! R2-D2 now looks just like he got pulled from the swamps of Dagobah!

R2-Q5

You can also turn R2-D2 into a whole other droid. This R2 unit worked for the Galactic Empire, serving aboard the second Death Star.

TIP: Since the main color of this model is black, the order of colors may seem backward. But it's important to follow the rule of lightest color to darkest. Again, paint all of the engraved pieces before assembling.

WHAT YOU NEED:
- Black, bronze, and silver paint
- Clear nail polish
- Tiny paint brush

OPTIONAL:
- Detail paintbrush (such as a 18/0 spotter)
- Small, flat bright brush (recommended 1/8'')
- Painter's or model tape

1. Paint in the silver where you want it to go.
2. Paint in the bronze where you want it to go.
3. Let both silver and bronze paints dry.
4. Paint in the black, being careful to edge around the silver and bronze details.
5. Once the engraved pieces are dry, assemble the model.
6. Paint the unfinished pieces of the model black.
7. Once the paint is dry, add bronze stripes to the front of each leg,
8. Finally, to get a glossy finish, paint the entire model with clear nail polish. Make sure to have an adult help you with this part.

R4-P17

There are plenty of droids in the galaxy that you can turn your model into. This astromech unit worked for Obi-Wan Kenobi and served him well through many battles.

WHAT YOU NEED:
- White, black, dark red, and silver paint
- Tiny paint brush

OPTIONAL:
- Detail paintbrush (such as a 18/0 spotter)
- Small, flat bright brush (recommended 1/8")
- Painter's or model tape

This model is very similar to the R2-D2 Replica project from page 29. Please refer to those instructions for this.

Remember, it's important to paint from lightest color to darkest. In this case, the order will be:

1) White, **2)** Silver, **3)** Red, **4)** Black

The last thing to add is a color for R4's front light. It changes colors frequently in the films, so you can decide what you want. A light blue was used in this example.

STAR WARS™

X-WING

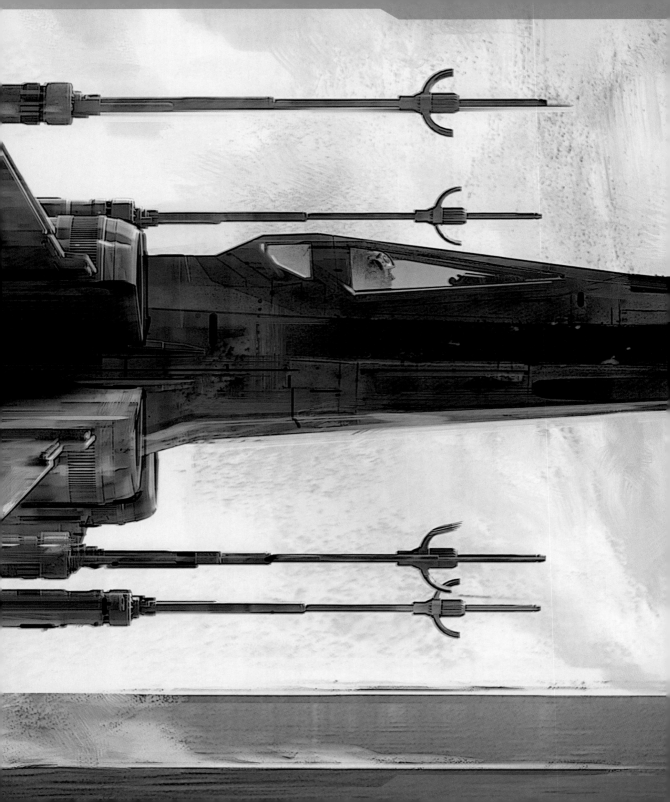

STAR WARS

X-WING

INSIDE THE GALAXY'S MOST VERSATILE STARFIGHTER

BY MICHAEL KOGGE

INCREDI
BUILDS

A Division of Insight Editions, LP
San Rafael, California

INTRODUCTION

In its fight against the evil Empire, the Rebel Alliance was always vastly outnumbered. It couldn't call on fleets of Star Destroyers to lead attacks. Nor could it deploy squadrons upon squadrons of TIE fighters without concern over losses. Despite this colossal imbalance, the Alliance did possess one asset the Empire lacked: a special weapon that destroyed thousands of TIEs, crippled more than a few Star Destroyers, and even atomized two Death Stars.

The rebels had the X-wing—a vehicle so versatile and deadly that many Alliance leaders readily admit that without it, the Empire would have crushed the Rebellion once and for all. Perhaps the greatest testament to the X-wing's success is its longevity. Decades after its introduction, the X-wing remains in service for the forces of the New Republic and the Resistance.

This one-man starfighter boasts a design as utilitarian as it is elegant. Its tapered nose expands into a long, narrow fuselage that encompasses a cockpit and droid slot before terminating in four S-foil wings, each equipped with laser cannons and powerful engines. To increase its firing range during combat runs, these S-foils open up in a crisscross pattern that gives the X-wing its name. Deflector shields and durasteel plating protect the fighter from enemy fire, while hyperspace motivators in each engine unit allow it to quickly enter or escape the field of battle. Moreover, the socketed astromech droid can perform repairs, compute astronavigational coordinates, and even operate the ship if necessary, giving X-wing pilots an edge over TIE fighter pilots, who lack such support.

Though it may not achieve the extreme speeds of the A-wing or carry the heavy ordnance of the Y-wing, the X-wing compensates by filling the middle ground between these two sister craft by being both fast and well armed, making it the ultimate, all-purpose starfighter. With a good pilot at its controls, the X-wing can tangle with TIE fighters as effectively as an A-wing or run a bombing campaign in place of a Y-wing. The Rebel Alliance, New Republic, and Resistance have all depended on this versatility to accomplish the most daring of missions, from long–distance reconnaissance to outflanking Imperial armadas.

T-65 X-WING

The original T-65 X-wing was the jack-of-all-trades in the Rebellion's starfighter fleet. Rugged yet agile and able to deliver quite a punch, it proved to be the sharpest thorn in the Imperial Navy's side.

TECHNICAL SPECIFICATIONS

MANUFACTURER: Incom Corporation

MODEL: T-65 X-wing

CLASS: Starfighter

WIDTH/HEIGHT/DEPTH:
11.46 m x 3.08 m x 13.31 m

WEAPONRY: Four laser cannons; two proton torpedo launchers

SHIELDS: Yes

MAXIMUM SPEED: 3,700 G (space) / 1,050 kph (atmosphere)

HYPERDRIVE: Class 1

LIFE SUPPORT SYSTEMS: Yes

CREW: 1 + astromech droid

CONSUMABLES: One-week supply

COST: 150,000 Imperial credits new; 90,000 used (military requisition charges)

INCOM GBK-585 HYPER-DRIVE MOTIVATOR (4): Built into the engine nacelles, all four form a hyperspace jump initiation circuit, equivalent to a hyperdrive with a Class 1 multiplier.

INCOM 4L4 FUSIAL THRUST ENGINES: Power converters, alluvial dampeners, turbo impellers, and lateral stabilizers make these some of the most efficient engines ever designed.

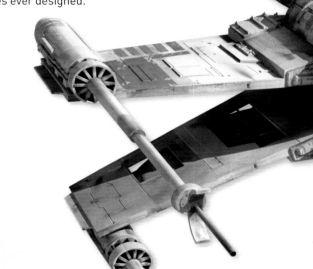

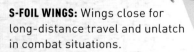

S-FOIL WINGS: Wings close for long-distance travel and unlatch in combat situations.

CARGO COMPARTMENT: A two-cubic-meter hold offers pilots a place to stash survival gear or special equipment for extended missions.

KRUPX MG7 PROTON TORPEDO LAUNCHER (2): Each launcher is loaded with a magazine of three torpedoes.

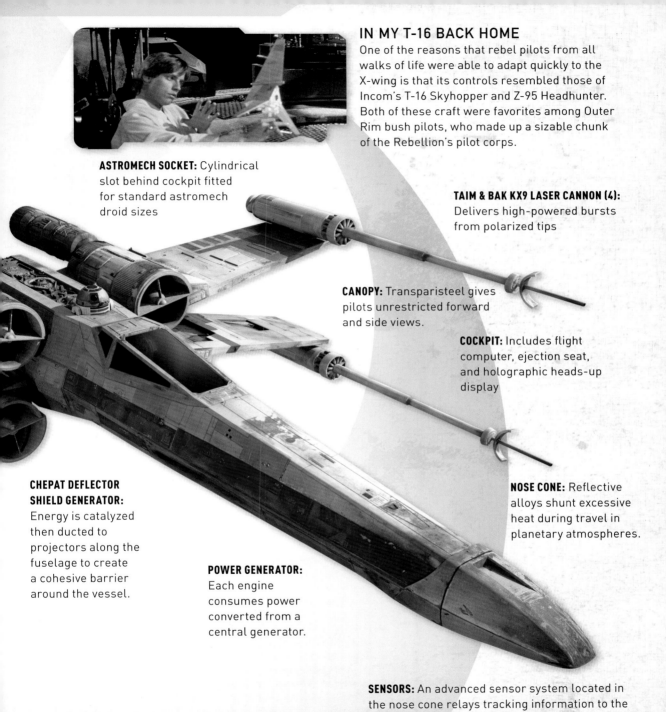

IN MY T-16 BACK HOME

One of the reasons that rebel pilots from all walks of life were able to adapt quickly to the X-wing is that its controls resembled those of Incom's T-16 Skyhopper and Z-95 Headhunter. Both of these craft were favorites among Outer Rim bush pilots, who made up a sizable chunk of the Rebellion's pilot corps.

ASTROMECH SOCKET: Cylindrical slot behind cockpit fitted for standard astromech droid sizes

TAIM & BAK KX9 LASER CANNON (4): Delivers high-powered bursts from polarized tips

CANOPY: Transparisteel gives pilots unrestricted forward and side views.

COCKPIT: Includes flight computer, ejection seat, and holographic heads-up display

CHEPAT DEFLECTOR SHIELD GENERATOR: Energy is catalyzed then ducted to projectors along the fuselage to create a cohesive barrier around the vessel.

POWER GENERATOR: Each engine consumes power converted from a central generator.

NOSE CONE: Reflective alloys shunt excessive heat during travel in planetary atmospheres.

SENSORS: An advanced sensor system located in the nose cone relays tracking information to the targeting computer while also collecting long-range data for reconnaissance.

FIERCE FIGHTER

The Empire and First Order learned the hard way not to underestimate the X-wing's capabilities. An X-wing may be slower and less maneuverable than a TIE, but its many other attributes—particularly its combat capability—make it the superior starfighter.

ARMED TO THE NOSE

The X-wing has double the laser weaponry found in a basic TIE, as each wing is armed with a long-barrel KX9 cannon. Pilots can unleash all four cannons at once, trigger individual cannons for precision shots, or fire any desired combination to maintain a constant barrage. Parabolic dishes around each polarized tip suppress possible "flashback" of excess energy that could melt the cannon.

PROTON PACKER

If laser cannons prove inadequate, an X-wing's proton torpedos can finish the job. When the target is properly locked, these energy missiles are able to pierce ray shields and inflict damage on a scale that few TIEs—and even moon-sized battle stations—can weather!

QUALITY VS. QUANTITY

The number of X-wings the rebels built during the Galactic Civil War paled compared to the hundreds of thousands of TIEs that Sienar Fleet Systems pumped out for the Empire. Nonetheless, because of Incom's engineers' insistence on using state-of-the-art componentry and hand-assembly techniques, the X-wing proved superior to the mass-produced Empire fighters. Constructing an X-wing cost more than double the price to construct a TIE, but its battle-survival rate was many times higher.

LOCK AND LOAD

When an X-wing enters a combat zone, two wings seemingly become four. Servos split the starfighter's S-foils to offer the pilot an expanded field of fire for its laser cannons. For faster travel, particularly in atmosphere and hyperspace, the S-foils collapse to reduce drag.

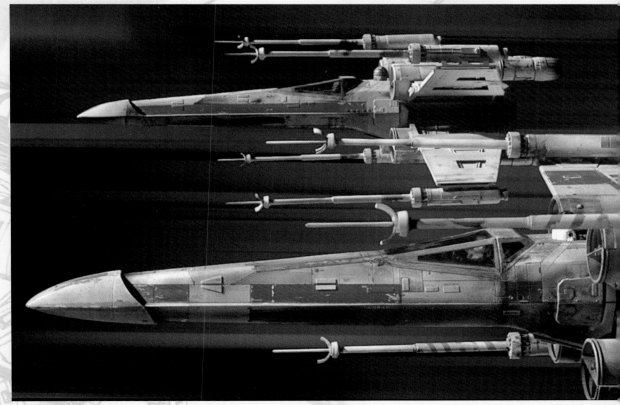

TOUGH TARGET

The X-wing's narrow shape makes it hard for enemy gunners to acquire a lock on it. Even then, a direct hit might fizzle against the X-wing's deflector shields or be absorbed by its reinforced titanium hull. Often TIE fighter pilots mistakenly believe they've downed their enemy only to have the X-wing withstand the TIE attack and respond with a barrage of its own.

AIM AID

The sensor array at the X-wing's nose pings the location of surrounding craft and transmits this information to the tracking computer and astro-mech droid. In conjunction, these machines calculate all available firing windows for the cockpit's heads-up display, where a simple three-dimensional wireframe view eschews visual distractions to focus on what's essential: the target.

RECON ROGUE

Space duels with TIE fighters are only one arena where the X-wing shines. It also serves as the ideal craft for reconnaissance, espionage, and rescue missions. Those who have the privilege of flying an X-wing must be able to leave the cockpit and perform daring ground operations that no TIE fighter pilot would ever be asked to do.

PETULANT PARTNER

Flesh-and-blood X-wing pilots are not alone in their endeavors. Plugged in behind every pilot is a robotic right hand—an astromech unit that monitors all the ship's instrumentation to ensure top performance. The droid can perform compli-cated navigation computations, execute repairs during combat, and even fly the X-wing if the pilot becomes incapacitated or just needs to rest on long journeys. Many pilots become attached to their assigned droids and refrain from wiping their memory banks, concerned that the droid might lose its special connection to them. Consequently, these astromechs can develop quirky personal-ities of their own and often become as cocky and brash as the pilots!

QUICK GETAWAYS

Unlike all standard TIE models, the X-wing is outfitted with the biggest lifesaver of all: a hyper-drive. The Class 1 unit permits travel to distant locales without the aid of a hyperdrive booster ring or being ferried by a capital ship. It also gives pilots the option to duck out of hopeless battles and live to fight another day.

SOLO SCOUT

The sensor system on the X-wing can be set for silent-passive or high-transmission-active mode, with the ability to scan wide or specify signatures and areas to narrow the search. The array at the nose of the craft gathers its data through a Carbanti universal transceiver that contains components for full-spectrum lock tracking, energy multi-imaging, and low-level terrain discernment. Both the Fabritech ANq sensor computers and astromech droid analyze the data and provide the pilot with their interpretations. Lone X-wing pilots are often tasked with jumping into enemy territory, collecting data about military targets, and jumping out before being noticed.

JAMMIN' AWAY

Sometimes the X-wing's most valuable defense isn't its deflector shields or hull, but the Betriak "Screamer" system that many craft possess. It creates noise on the electromagnetic spectrum that can confuse the tracking systems of TIE fighters or seeker missiles.

T-70 X-WING

The T-70 X-wing adheres to the old engineering axiom that "if it ain't broke, don't fix it." Built decades after the T-65, it retains much of its predecessor's classic design, with some minor enhancements that ensure it remains the superior starfighter in the galaxy.

TECHNICAL SPECIFICATIONS

MANUFACTURER: Incom Corporation

MODEL: T-70 X-wing

CLASS: Starfighter

WIDTH/HEIGHT/DEPTH: 12.49 m x 11.26 m x 2.73 m

WEAPONRY: Four laser cannons;
two proton torpedo launchers

SHIELDS: Yes

MAXIMUM SPEED: 3,800 G (space) / 1,100 kph (atmosphere)

HYPERDRIVE: Class 1

LIFE SUPPORT SYSTEMS: Yes

CREW: 1 + astromech droid

CONSUMABLES: One-week supply

COST: 210,000 Republic credits new;
120,000 used (military requisition charges)

BLACK ONE

Resistance pilot Poe Dameron's customized T-70 X-wing sports a black ferrosphere paint coat that scatters the pings of enemy sensors, making it harder to hit.

SENSORS: An advanced linked system throughout the cone relays tracking information to the targeting computer while also permitting long-range data collection for reconnaissance.

SCARCE STARFIGHTERS

The Resistance finds itself in the same conundrum as the former Rebel Alliance in acquiring an ample supply of X-wings. New Republic demilitarization policies, along with starship trade monopolies, have forced the Resistance to rely on wealthy donors sympathetic to its cause to maintain its small starfighter corps.

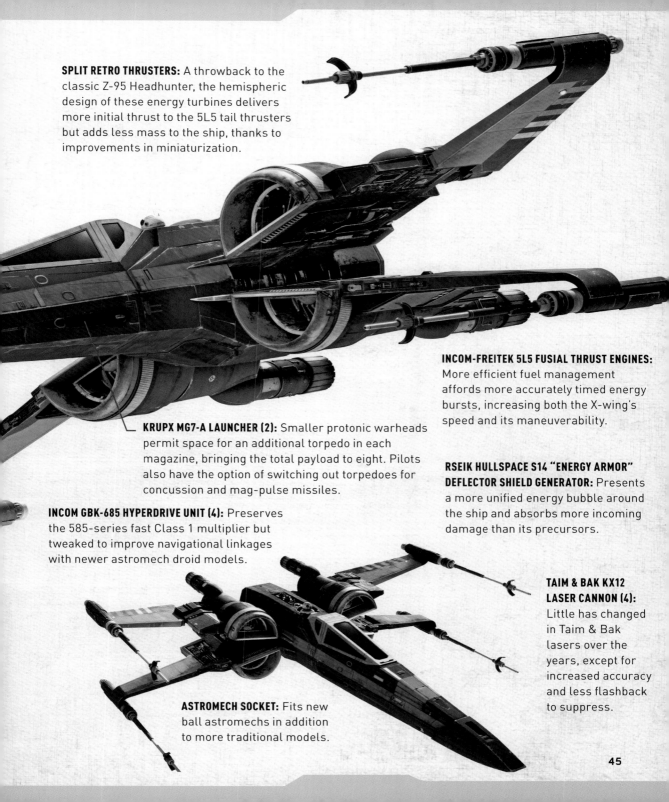

SPLIT RETRO THRUSTERS: A throwback to the classic Z-95 Headhunter, the hemispheric design of these energy turbines delivers more initial thrust to the 5L5 tail thrusters but adds less mass to the ship, thanks to improvements in miniaturization.

INCOM-FREITEK 5L5 FUSIAL THRUST ENGINES: More efficient fuel management affords more accurately timed energy bursts, increasing both the X-wing's speed and its maneuverability.

KRUPX MG7-A LAUNCHER (2): Smaller protonic warheads permit space for an additional torpedo in each magazine, bringing the total payload to eight. Pilots also have the option of switching out torpedoes for concussion and mag-pulse missiles.

RSEIK HULLSPACE S14 "ENERGY ARMOR" DEFLECTOR SHIELD GENERATOR: Presents a more unified energy bubble around the ship and absorbs more incoming damage than its precursors.

INCOM GBK-685 HYPERDRIVE UNIT (4): Preserves the 585-series fast Class 1 multiplier but tweaked to improve navigational linkages with newer astromech droid models.

TAIM & BAK KX12 LASER CANNON (4): Little has changed in Taim & Bak lasers over the years, except for increased accuracy and less flashback to suppress.

ASTROMECH SOCKET: Fits new ball astromechs in addition to more traditional models.

BIG SHOTS

Though many have flown in the cockpit of an X-wing, two pilots stand out in the course of galactic history: Luke Skywalker and Poe Dameron.

LUKE SKYWALKER, REBEL PILOT

Luke spent his teenage years racing T-16 Skyhoppers through Beggar's Canyon on Tatooine, so he had little trouble grasping the X-wing's controls or flying down the trench of the Death Star.

POE DAMERON, RESISTANCE PILOT

Poe grew up the son of Shara Bey, an A-wing pilot who fought in the Battle of Endor, so he had a jump start from an early age in learning how to fly starfighters.

Lost Ship

During Poe's mission to retrieve an important artifact on Jakku, the First Order destroyed his X-wing and took Poe prisoner aboard its Star Destroyer. Since the Resistance possessed very few starfighters, the loss of even one was costly. Fortunately, Poe escaped the Star Destroyer in a TIE fighter and was able to jump back into a T-70 cockpit to help turn the tide against the First Order at Takodana.

POE DAMERON, RESISTANCE PILOT

Poe grew up the son of Shara Bey, an A-wing pilot who fought in the Battle of Endor, so he had a jump start from an early age in learning how to fly starfighters.

Lost Ship

During Poe's mission to retrieve an important artifact on Jakku, the First Order destroyed his X-wing and took Poe prisoner aboard its Star Destroyer. Since the Resistance possessed very few starfighters, the loss of even one was costly. Fortunately, Poe escaped the Star Destroyer in a TIE fighter and was able to jump back into a T-70 cockpit to help turn the tide against the First Order at Takodana.

Ace Command

For starfighter engagements in which secrecy isn't mandated, Poe flies a customized black T-70 with orange racing stripes known as *Black One*. He captained both Red and Blue Squadrons as "Black Leader" in the battles of Takodana and Starkiller Base, where his high-flying skills and expert leadership saved many pilots' lives and contributed to the Resistance's biggest victory— the destruction of the Starkiller superweapon.

PILOTS OF THE REBELLION

Countless men and women dedicated their lives as Rebel Alliance X-wing pilots to liberate the galaxy from the shackles of the Empire.

BIGGS DARKLIGHTER

Biggs and his best friend, Luke Skywalker, both dreamed of entering the Imperial Academy to train as pilots, but only Darklighter left Tatooine to do so. His time as an Imperial was short-lived, and not long after graduation he defected to the Rebellion. His path crossed with Skywalker's for a final time at the Battle of Yavin, during which the two flew as wingmates. Darklighter perished in the Death Star trenches under Darth Vader's lasers, but his sacrifice allowed Skywalker to trigger the shot that destroyed the Death Star.

WEDGE ANTILLES

One of the few surviving Rebel pilots at the Battle of Yavin, Wedge went on to have a stellar career for the Rebellion and New Republic. He flew a snowspeeder for Rogue Group during the Imperial assault on Hoth to help his rebel comrades evacuate their base. At the Battle of Endor, he commanded Red Squadron and led the charge alongside the *Millennium Falcon* into the Death Star's superstructure.

JEK PORKINS

Porkins had a storied flight record, having accomplished many missions for the Rebellion. Sadly, "Red Six" was one of the first X-wing pilots lost at the Battle of Yavin. The memory of him, however, continued to burn bright in the hearts of rebels for years afterward.

PILOTS OF THE RESISTANCE

A new generation of X-wing pilots fights for the Resistance against the oppressive First Order.

JESSIKA PAVA

Youth is not a limiting factor for Pava; she puts many of the older, more experienced Resistance pilots to shame. When flying X-wings, she's "Blue Three" of Blue Squadron, though on the ground her friends just call her "Jess" or "Testor."

NIEN NUNB

Famed for copiloting the *Millennium Falcon* with Lando Calrissian at the Battle of Endor, Nien Nunb refused to retire from the cockpit, especially when tyranny was on the march yet again. The Resistance was overjoyed to have in their ranks this brave Sullustan, who's capable of flying just about anything with an engine.

TEMMIN "SNAP" WEXLEY

Born on Akiva to parents who had ties to the Rebellion, Wexley later followed in their footsteps and joined the Resistance. His reconnaissance flight targeting Starkiller Base provided the Resistance with the intelligence necessary to formulate an attack to destroy it. Captain Wexley gladly participated in that attack as a member of Blue Squadron under Poe Dameron's command.

X-WING BATTLES

During the war against the Galactic Empire, rebel X-wing pilots braved overwhelming odds to help put an end to tyranny. With the First Order on the rise, the Resistance now continues the fight one battle at a time.

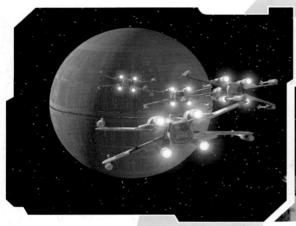

BATTLE OF YAVIN

When the Death Star threatened to obliterate the Rebel Alliance's hidden base on Yavin 4, just thirty starfighters were mobilized to protect the planet. Grand Moff Tarkin, the battle station's overseer, deemed the rebels' response trivial, and did not bother to launch TIE squadrons to intercept the X-wings. Only Darth Vader acknowledged the danger the rebels posed, and if not for one X-wing pilot gifted in the Force, Vader and his TIE squadron would have driven off the rebels, and Yavin 4 would have met the same fiery fate as Alderaan.

BATTLE OF ENDOR

Admiral Ackbar's daring plan was to bring the entire Rebel Alliance fleet to Endor in a surprise attack on the Emperor's second Death Star. The rebels sent just about every X-wing they possessed into a war zone thick with TIE fighters and Star Destroyers. Many gave their lives just to buy time for the rebel commandos on the forest moon who were trying to destroy the Death Star's shield generator. When the shields came down, a couple of X-wings accompanied the *Millennium Falcon* through the labyrinth of the Death Star's superstructure and helped detonate the power core. It proved the turning point in toppling the Galactic Empire.

BATTLE OF TAKODANA

Alerted that BB-8 was in Maz Kanata's castle on Takodana, the Resistance sent a small force to rescue the ball-shaped droid and the vital information he carried. A squadron of T-70 X-wings led the attack, plummeting through the atmosphere and skimming over the opalescent surface of Takodana's lakes. They found the First Order had already beaten them to the planet and had leveled the castle to smoking ruins. When the X-wings arrived, the First Order quickly turned tail and retreated to space, taking with it not BB-8 but another prisoner: a tech scavenger from Jakku named Rey.

BATTLE OF STARKILLER BASE

After annihilating the New Republic capital of Hosnian Prime and its fleet, First Order General Hux aimed his Starkiller weapon at the Resistance base on D'Qar. The Resistance scrambled what few X-wings it had in a desperate attempt to destroy the superweapon's core before it destroyed them. Red and Blue Squadrons fought valiantly in the skies of Starkiller Base while a Resistance team on the ground planted explosives inside the bomb-proof oscillator. The resulting explosion breached the oscillator, permitting Poe to fly into the energy containment system and destroy it with proton torpedoes, sparking the implosion of Starkiller Base.

BEHIND THE SCENES

"I wanted a dragster with a long narrow front and a guy sitting on the back."

—*Star Wars* creator George Lucas on his inspiration for the X-wing

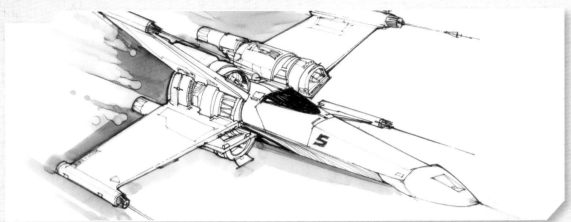

SIX SHOOTER

Colin Cantwell, the *2001: A Space Odyssey* photographic effects specialist George Lucas hired to design the *Star Wars* starships, came up with the idea of opening the wings for the rebel starfighter. He likened the splitting of the S-foils to that of a Western gunslinger drawing his revolver.

ARTISTS' ALLEY

The X-wing was the brainchild of Cantwell and Lucas, but a number of artists contributed to its final design. Joe Johnston revised the starfighter in additional concept sketches, giving it flat canopy windows to minimize reflections during filming. Steve Gawley then made orthographic drawings, adding mechanical details and labeling various components. Finally, Grant McCune and his team at the Industrial Light & Magic (ILM) model shop made practical adjustments, like finding an appropriately shaped snub nose for the ship, during construction of the miniatures.

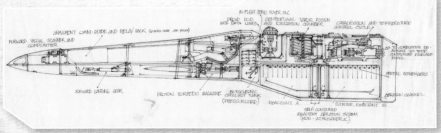

IT'S ELECTRIC!

The X-wing wasn't just any plastic model. The S-foil wings could open and close via a motor. Lightbulbs in each exhaust nacelle created the blue engine glow. Fiber-optic tips allowed the laser cannons to "blink." And to make sure the model didn't burn up, cooling lines of surgical tubing were snaked inside the X-wing's frame.

RED FOR A REASON

George Lucas's screenplay for the initial *Star Wars* film designated the X-wings as "Blue Squadron" and their sister craft, the Y-wings, as "Red Squadron." However, shooting against a blue screen made it impossible for the models to be blue because those parts would blend into the background and disappear on screen. As a consequence, the X-wings had their racing stripes painted red.

PARTS ARE PARTS

Spaceship builders at ILM recycled pieces from model kits for German World War II tanks, Kandy-Vans, Ford Galaxie 500/XLs, and Revell racers to manufacture miniature X-wings and other *Star Wars* starfighters.

FLYBY KNIGHTS

When X-wings flew close to the camera in dogfights with TIE fighters, sound designer Ben Burtt used artillery sounds from the classic movie *The Guns of Navarone* and mixed in a lion's roar or a thunderclap for extra punch and rumble.

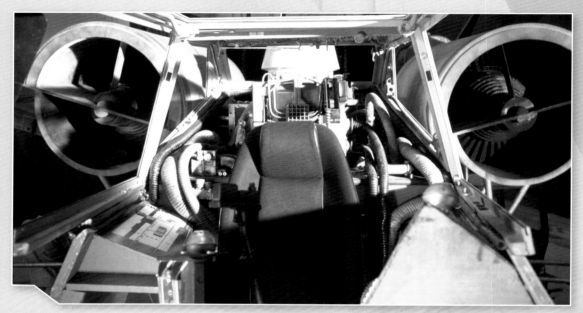

HOT SEAT

All the shots of Luke and the other X-wing pilots were filmed using the same life-size cockpit at Elstree Studios. Former NASA spacecraft designer Harry Lange decorated the set, installing the lights, buttons, switches, and panels to make the console look like that of a real spaceship.

ONLY ONE THERE IS

The original *Star Wars* production budgeted a single, practical X-wing to be built at England's Shepperton Studios, where the throne room and rebel base hangar scenes were shot. Other life-size X-wings were paintings, draped into the shot as backdrops or composited to the film negative during postproduction.

AERIAL ACROBATICS

George Lucas assembled a 16-millimeter reel of film clips featuring World War II fighter planes dipping and weaving around each other to show the aeronautics he envisioned for the Death Star space battle between X-wings and TIE fighters in *Star Wars*.

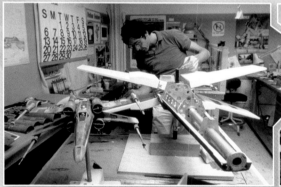

FRENCH CONNECTIONS

ILM head John Dykstra and his team pioneered motion control techniques and cameras to film the model spaceships. He was determined to make the last reel of *Star Wars* "as exciting as the car chase in *The French Connection*."

BIGGER AND BETTER

For *Return of the Jedi*, model maker Mike Fulmer constructed a "hero version" of the X-wing that, at four feet, was many times larger than the other models. ILM photographed a sweeping flyby close-up of Luke and R2-D2 in the fighter, but the shot was left on the cutting room floor. The model, however, remains a popular attraction in museum tours of *Star Wars* artifacts.

DASHBOARD DREAMS

The Force Awakens production team provided actor Oscar Isaac (Poe Dameron) with a blueprint of his X-wing's console to help make his performance as a starfighter pilot as authentic as possible. It listed the proper steps for a launch sequence, which controls had been used in previous films, and all the new buttons he could press to make up his own flight patterns.

ABOVE: In a single frame, production artist Ralph McQuarrie captures the speed and danger of an X-wing streaking down the confines of the Death Star trench while being harassed by laser fire.

ABOVE: Not yet fully trained in the Force, Luke Skywalker uses a long pole to try to push his starfighter out of the Dagobah bog, to no avail. Production painting by Ralph McQuarrie.

ABOVE: A Resistance X-wing skims over the lakes of Takodana to surprise the First Order forces that have launched a raid on Maz Kanata's castle. Concept art by Kevin Jenkins.

BELOW: The X-wings of the Resistance's Red and Blue Squadrons descend into a vicious swarm of First Order TIE fighters as they attempt to destroy the central oscillator on Starkiller Base. Concept art by James Clyne.

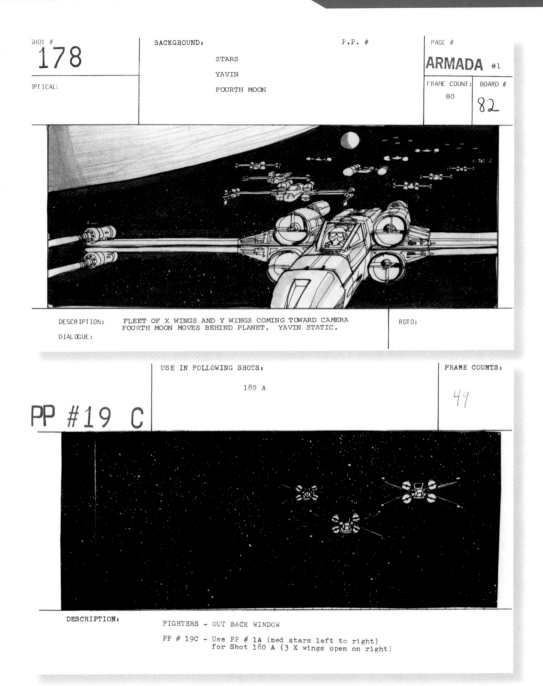

DESCRIPTION: FLEET OF X WINGS AND Y WINGS COMING TOWARD CAMERA
FOURTH MOON MOVES BEHIND PLANET.   YAVIN STATIC.

DIALOGUE: ROTO:

USE IN FOLLOWING SHOTS: FRAME COUNTS:

180 A   49

PP #19 C

DESCRIPTION:

FIGHTERS - OUT BACK WINDOW

PP # 19C - Use PP # 1A (med stars left to right)
             for Shot 180 A (3 X wings open on right)

This storyboard sequence provided the miniature effects team with a visual guide for the iconic scene in which the X-wings approach the first Death Star and "lock S-foils in attack position." These heavily detailed drawings ensured that time was not wasted on producing sequences that were not necessary to the film.

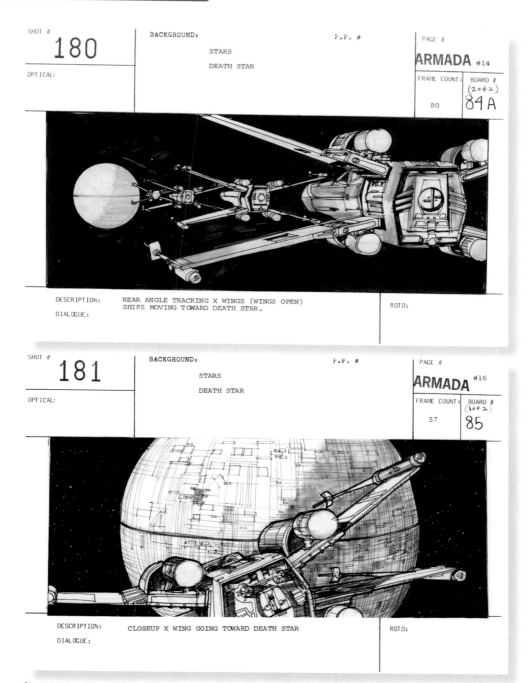

SHOT #

180

OPTICAL:

BACKGROUND:

STARS

DEATH STAR

P.P. #

PAGE #

ARMADA #14

FRAME COUNT: BOARD #
                        (20 ¢ 2)
        80   84A

DESCRIPTION: REAR ANGLE TRACKING X WINGS (WINGS OPEN)
                        SHIPS MOVING TOWARD DEATH STAR.
DIALOGUE:

ROTO:

SHOT #

181

OPTICAL:

BACKGROUND:

STARS

DEATH STAR

P.P. #

PAGE #

ARMADA #16

FRAME COUNT: BOARD #
                        (10 ¢ 2)
        57   85

DESCRIPTION: CLOSEUP X WING GOING TOWARD DEATH STAR
DIALOGUE:

ROTO:

Since the shots that were filmed often required weeks—if not months—of model-making, motion control photography, and postproduction compositing, preplanning was essential.

INTERVIEW WITH RICHARD EDLUND

Richard Edlund is one of the pioneers of modern motion picture special effects. He served as the first cameraman for the miniature and optical effects units on *Star Wars* and contributed to the visual and special effects for *The Empire Strikes Back*, *Return of the Jedi*, and *Raiders of the Lost Ark*, all of which won Academy Awards for Edlund and the effects team at Industrial Light & Magic. He founded Boss Film Studios in 1983, where he oversaw the visual and computer effects on films like *Ghostbusters*, *2010: The Year We Make Contact*, and *Air Force One*. He continues to be involved in the industry today, producing his own pictures at Richard Edlund Films.

WHAT FIRST INTERESTED YOU IN SPECIAL EFFECTS?

I went to the USC School of Cinematic Arts when I got out of the Navy. I didn't want to burden my parents, so I decided to get a job. I wound up getting a job with Joe Westheimer. He had an optical house. We did special effects for commercials, TV shows, and a few features. I became a hippie photographer for a couple of years, then got back into the business with Bob Abel. We were doing multipass, very complicated but really beautiful television commercials, like the Butterfly Girl for 7-Up and [also their] "Uncola" campaign.

HOW DID YOU GET INVOLVED IN *STAR WARS*?

I was called by [Industrial Light & Magic head] John Dykstra one day to come out and talk about the possibility of being a cameraman for the *Star Wars* effects unit. Anybody who's in TV wants to do features, and *Star Wars* was a big 20th Century Fox sci-fi movie. I started with a phone and a card table in this huge room in an industrial warehouse building. We had to build the entire photographic system—optical printers, cameras, the motion control equipment, the electronics—from scratch.

WHAT WERE YOUR PRIMARY CONTRIBUTIONS TO *STAR WARS*?

I knew photographic systems backward and forward, I understood the chemistry, I understood the mechanics, optics, and all those kind of things. What I needed to do on *Star Wars* was to design the camera, the camera system, and how we would shoot the miniatures. The boom, the underslung camera, the Trojan helmet moto-point pan-tilt head the camera was situated in, and coming up with ideas to build optical printers—all that stuff was me.

When George came back from shooting in England, I spent about a week with him programming shots, shooting tests, and running the black-and-white tests. I had to teach George how we were going to be able use the system we built. And, like any system, it had limitations.

CAN YOU DESCRIBE THE SYSTEM YOU DEVISED TO SHOOT THE X-WING STARFIGHTERS AND OTHER MINIATURES?

We had twelve channels of motion control, each one of which had to be programmed separately. I had to program the track move, the pan, the tilt, the roll, the swing, the boom, and then the model itself had to be programmed. All of these things had to be done in sequence, because I didn't want to crash the model or crash the camera into the model. I even had a contact mic on the boom so I could hear these various overtones of the motors, which gave me a clue as to how fast I was going with the camera.

HOW DID YOU MANAGE TO SHOOT MULTIPLE X-WINGS IN ONE SHOT?

The thing is, in *Star Wars* we had so many elements to shoot—there were thousands of elements involved in putting in the compositing. And most of the X-wings were shot separately. I would run a shot of an X-wing through the Moviola film editor with the take of the next X-wing that was supposed to be in the shot. I would bipack [combine] those in the Moviola and see how they worked together. Once I did the first test and it looked good, I'd shoot the beauty pass of the X-wing against blue screen. Then I had to break that setup down.

WHAT WERE SOME CHALLENGES YOU FACED WHILE FILMING THE CLIMACTIC DEATH STAR TRENCH BATTLE?

We discovered that in running the camera down the trench, the camera could only shoot the first forty feet of it. I had to figure out how to use forced perspective paintings at the end of the trench. I'd line the shots up so that I could do three runs down the trench with the camera and then seamlessly join the other two shots, the end of one to the beginning of the next. Sometimes we'd have to project things through the camera to line them up. It was a lot of seat-of-the-pants work. You'd have to do a test and see how it worked. If you got it almost right, you tweaked it a little bit and you got it better, and then you go for it, you shoot it.

DID SOME OF THE X-WING MODELS SUFFER BATTLE DAMAGE OF THEIR OWN?

In order to get the dynamics of the movie that George needed, I was virtually scraping the model with the camera. Sometimes I'd break the tip off an X-wing's laser and have to call the model shop to come out and fix it!

MAKE IT YOUR OWN

One of the great things about IncrediBuilds models is that each one is completely customizable. The untreated natural wood can be decorated with paints, pencils, pens—the list goes on and on!

Before you start building and decorating your model, read through the included instruction sheet so you understand how all the pieces come together. Then, choose a theme and make a plan. Do you want to make an exact replica of an X-wing or create something completely wacky? The choice is yours! Here are some sample projects to get those creative juices flowing.

Every X-wing has its own droid. You can make these any color you like.

For a simple stand, paint it black. Then use a silver permanent marker to outline the base.

T-65B X-WING

Re-create the iconic starfighter that carried the rebels to victory over the Death Star in *A New Hope*. When making a replica, it's always good to study an actual image of what you are trying to copy. Look closely at the details found in this book and brainstorm how you can re-create them.

WHAT YOU NEED
- Matte white acrylic paint
- Yellow, gray, blue, and red paint
- Pencil
- Gray chalk pastel
- Cotton swab

WHAT YOU MIGHT WANT
- Piece of sandpaper
- Detail brush (18/0 size or smaller)
- Silver permanent marker

1. Assemble the model, but leave the wings, laser cannons, and stand off.
2. Paint the assembled model white.
3. Separately, paint the wings and laser cannons white.
4. Add coats of paint as needed. **TIP: Use sandpaper in between coats of paint for a smoother finish.**
5. Once the pieces are dry, paint the yellow details onto the main model, the wings, and the laser cannons. Let dry.
6. Paint the back of the engines and the deflector shield generator gray. Then add the gray details to the wings. **TIP: To create a gradient (from dark to light), use a graphite pencil for the shading.**
7. Paint the red stripe on both sides of the ship.
8. Add the red details to the wings. The red stripes at the top of the wings are the call sign for the ship. You can add more or fewer stripes to denote different X-wings. Five red stripes make it Luke Skywalker's. This example is Red Four, piloted by John D. Branon during the battle of Yavin.
9. Assemble the model.
10. To finish, rub chalk pastel—using a cotton swab—around the ship to add some weathering.

CRASH LANDING!

On a mission to find Master Yoda, Luke Skywalker and R2-D2 find their X-wing sinking beneath the swamps of Dagobah. Yoda masterfully uses his knowledge of the Force to retrieve the X-wing for them. Re-create the X-wing that emerges from the swamp in *The Empire Strikes Back* with this project.

WHAT YOU NEED

- White, yellow, gray, red, black, brown, and green paint
- Paintbrush

WHAT YOU MIGHT WANT

- Detail brush (18/0 size or smaller)
- Two or more shades of green paint
- Two or more shades of brown paint
- White colored pencil
- Red colored pencil
- Light blue paint

TIP:
Adding black or white to a color will change its shade.

1. Start by creating a replica X-wing using steps 1 through 10 of the T-65B X-wing instructions. Remember to add five stripes of red to indicate that this is Luke Skywalker's X-wing.

2. Using the brown paint, start dabbing "dirt" onto the X-wing. Use your paintbrush to blend it in with the background color until you get the effect you want. If you have more than two shades of brown, start with the darker brown and use the lighter shade next.

3. Add the swampy greenery. Using dark green paint, paint green lines that drape around the ship. Go back and add rounded leaf shapes to those lines. To get more depth, go back and add lighter green to some.

4. Repeat steps 2 and 3 until you like how swampy it looks.

FOR A DIFFERENT EFFECT, color the pieces with white colored pencil before you assemble. Add the red stripe in colored pencil as well. You will paint over them next, but the pencil underneath creates more texture. It will also require fewer coats of paint!

THE SWAMPY STAND:

1. Paint the stand gray. Don't let the paint dry.

2. Wet your paintbrush and use light blue paint to create a wash over the gray stand.

3. Wiggle your paintbrush from the center of the stand toward the edge to create ripples.

4. Add more white to the top of the stand for fog. Blend well with the existing gray.

5. Use a small paintbrush to paint a green outline around the stand. The line shouldn't be neat and straight. Instead paint more rounded shapes to give the look of trees and bushes.

SOURCES (X-WING)

Bouzereau, Laurent. *Star Wars: The Annotated Screenplays.* New York: Del Rey, 1997.

Bray, Adam, Cole Horton, Kerrie Dougherty, and Michael Kogge. *Star Wars: Absolutely Everything You Need to Know.* New York: Dorling Kindersley, 2015.

Fry, Jason. *Star Wars: The Phantom Menace – The Expanded Visual Dictionary.* New York: Dorling Kindersley, 2012.

Hidalgo, Pablo. "The History of R-Series Astromech Droids." *Star Wars Adventure Journal* Vol. 7. August 1995. Honesdale, PA: West End Games. 129-143.

Johnson, Shane. *Star Wars: Technical Journal* Vol. 1. Starlog Magazine Presents, 1993.

Peterson, Lorne. *Sculpting a Galaxy.* San Rafael, CA: Insight Editions, 2006.

Reynolds, David West, James Luceno, and Ryder Windham. *The Complete Star Wars Visual Dictionary.* New York: Dorling Kindersley, 2006.

Rinzler, J.W. *Star Wars: The Blueprints.* Seattle, WA: 47North, 2013.

———. *The Making of Star Wars: The Definitive Story Behind the Film.* New York: Del Rey, 2007.

———. *The Making of Star Wars: Revenge of the Sith.* New York: Del Rey, 2005.

Wallace, Daniel. *The Essential Guide to Droids.* New York: Del Rey, 1999.

———. *The New Essential Guide to Droids.* New York: Del Rey, 2006.

SOURCES (R2-D2)

Blackman, Haden. *Star Wars: The New Essential Guide to Vehicles and Vessels.* New York: Del Rey, 2003.

Bray, Adam, Cole Horton, Kerrie Dougherty, and Michael Kogge. *Star Wars: Absolutely Everything You Need to Know.* New York: Dorling Kindersley, 2015.

Bouzereau, Laurent. *Star Wars: The Annotated Screenplays.* New York: Del Rey, 1997.

Dougherty, Kerrie, Hans Jessen, Curtis Saxton, David West Reynolds, and Ryder Windham. *Star Wars: Complete Vehicles.* New York: Dorling Kindersley, 2013.

Fry, Jason. *Star Wars: The Force Awakens Incredible Cross-Sections.* New York: Dorling Kindersley, 2015.

Hidalgo, Pablo. *Star Wars: The Force Awakens: The Visual Dictionary.* New York: Dorling Kindersley, 2015.

Murphy, Paul. *Star Wars: The Rebel Alliance Sourcebook.* Honesdale, PA: West End Games, 1990.

Peterson, Lorne. *Sculpting a Galaxy.* San Rafael, CA: Insight Editions, 2006.

Rinzler, J.W. *The Making of Star Wars: The Definitive Story Behind the Original Film.* New York: Del Rey, 2007.

———. *The Sounds of Star Wars.* San Francisco: Chronicle, 2010.

———. *Star Wars: The Blueprints.* Seattle: 47North, 2013.

Slavicsek, Bill and Curtis Smith. *The Star Wars Sourcebook.* Honesdale, PA: West End Games, 1987.

Smith, Bill. *Star Wars: The Essential Guide to Vehicles and Vessels.* New York: Del Rey, 1996.

Windham, Ryder. S*tar Wars: Millennium Falcon Owner's Workshop Manual.* New York: Del Rey, 2011.

ABOUT THE AUTHOR

MICHAEL KOGGE'S other recent work includes *Empire of the Wolf*, an epic graphic novel featuring werewolves in ancient Rome, and the Star Wars Rebels series of books. He resides online at www.MichaelKogge.com, while his real home is in Los Angeles.

IncrediBuilds™
A Division of Insight Editions LP
PO Box 3088
San Rafael, CA 94912
www.insighteditions.com

Find us on Facebook: www.facebook.com/InsightEditions

Follow us on Twitter: @insighteditions

© & ™ 2017 LUCASFILM LTD. Used Under Authorization.

Published by Insight Editions, San Rafael, California, in 2017. All rights reserved. No part of this book may be reproduced in any form without written permission from the publisher.

Library of Congress Cataloging-in-Publication Data available.

ISBN: 978-1-68298-158-0

Publisher: Raoul Goff
Associate Publisher: Vanessa Lopez
Art Director: Chrissy Kwasnik
Senior Editor: Chris Prince
Managing Editor: Molly Glover
Production Editors: Elaine Ou and Carly Chillmon
Associate Editor: Katie DeSandro
Editorial Assistant: Holly Fisher
Production Manager: Anna Wan and Thomas Chung
Associate Production Manager: Sam Taylor
Product Development Manager: Rebekah Piatte
Model Design: (R2-D2) He Jianzhu, Team Green
Model Design: (X-wing) Ryan Zhang and Ball Cheung, Team Green
Craft Photography: (R2-D2) Anthony Piatte

INSIGHT EDITIONS would like to thank Curt Baker, Leland Chee, Pablo Hidalgo, Samantha Holland, Daniel Saeva, and Krista Wong.

ROOTS of PEACE   REPLANTED PAPER

Insight Editions, in association with Roots of Peace, will plant two trees for each tree used in the manufacturing of this book. Roots of Peace is an internationally renowned humanitarian organization dedicated to eradicating land mines worldwide and converting war-torn lands into productive farms and wildlife habitats. Roots of Peace will plant two million fruit and nut trees in Afghanistan and provide farmers there with the skills and support necessary for sustainable land use.

Manufactured in China

10 9 8 7 6 5 4 3 2 1